Anniranni and Mollymishi

the Wild-Haired Doll

Story by C. Drew Lamm
Art by Ruth Ohi

Annick Press

Annick Press Ltd. Toronto

Annick Press gratefully acknowledges the support of The Canada Council and the Ontario Arts Council

Canadian Cataloguing in Publication Data

Lamm, C. Drew.
Anniranni and Mollymishi, the wildhaired doll

ISBN 1-55037-105-3 (bound).—ISBN 1-55037-106-1 (pbk.)

I. Ohi, Ruth. II. Title.

PS8573.A55A73 1990 jC813'.54 C90-093444-1
PZ7.L35An 1990

Distribution for Canada and the USA:

Firefly Books Ltd., 250 Sparks Avenue,
North York, Ontario M2H 2S4

Printed and bound in Canada
by D.W. Friesen & Sons

To Constance Margaret
E. Sculler and E. Bruce
Now-Then- Mr. Savage
Maxwell (my Mom and Dad)
and always to Steve

One day Anniranni and her wild-haired doll, Mollymishi, set off in Anniranni's wee red wagon. They rode down the steep street together and then Anniranni dragged them up the steep uphill, other-side.

At the top of the steep uphill, other-side, played a bunch of wild-eyed friends. Anniranni left Mollymishi in the wee red wagon while she ran over to investigate.

Mollymishi leaned over to look out the back of the wagon. Her weight shifted the wee red wagon backwards down the steep hill. Mollymishi and the wee red wagon sped down the hill.

In the middle of the hill the wee red wagon's shiny silver wheels caught on a crack.

The wee red wagon veered into the Vevverly's drive-way and careened around the corner of the house. It didn't stop until the shiny silver wheels caught on a clump of grass.

Mollymishi lurched forward as the wee red wagon came to an abrupt stop.

In front of Mollymishi there was a garden. Daffodils dangled above the grasses. Someone had left a blue shoed doll slumped on a stool. A butterfly landed on Mollymishi's dress. A sprinkle of sparrows pecked around the shiny silver wheels of the wee red wagon.

Mollymishi watched everything with her wide doll eyes. She sat quite content until the back screen door of the Vevverly's house slamwammed and a wild-eyed child and a brown-eyed dog ran straight toward Mollymishi.

"Come Dillip," said the wild-eyed child to the dog, and lifted Mollymishi out of the wee red wagon.

He tied Dillip's leash around Mollymishi's small doll hand.

Mollymishi rode on Dillip's hairly-furly back in circles around and around the daffodils until her hair stuck straight out in the sun.

Suddenly Dillip, the dog, saw a small Persian cat. He skidded past the wagon and after that cat. Mollymishi shot off his hairly-furly back and . . .

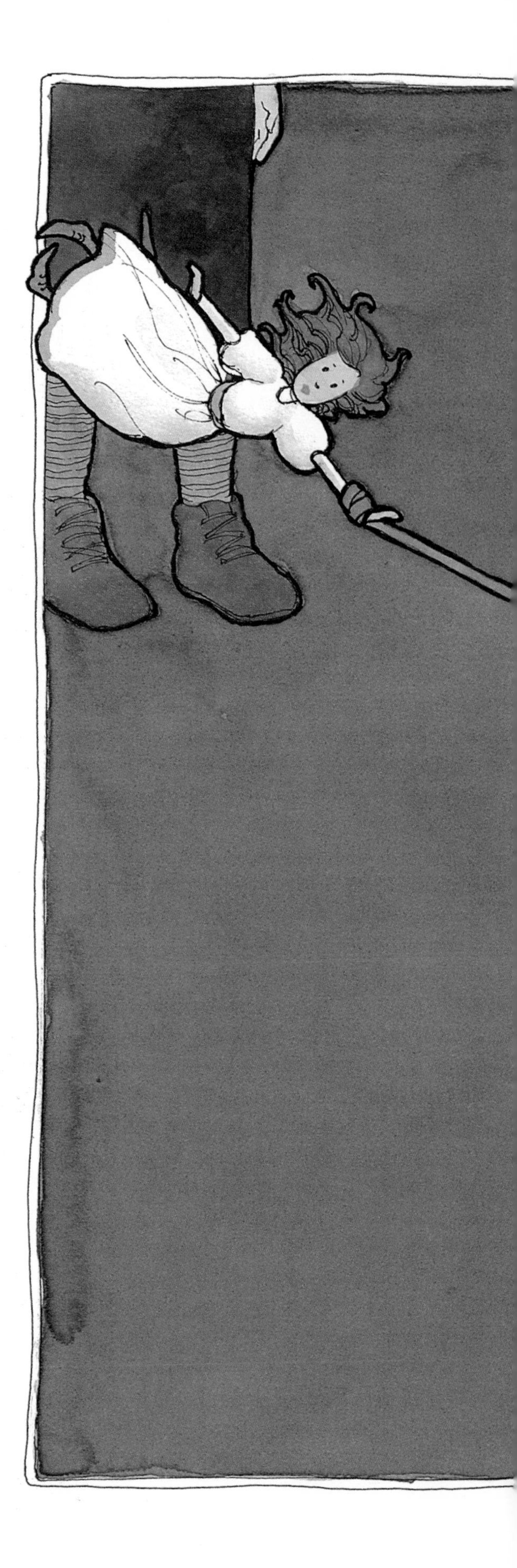

. . . landed in the wee red wagon. But, she still had one doll hand caught in Dillip's leash.

Back at the top of the steep uphill, other-side, Anniranni ran to where her wagon had been. It was gone! Anniranni ran and ran up and down the whole live long hill. She couldn't find the wee red wagon or Mollymishi, her wild-haired doll anywhere. Finally Anniranni sat down at the bottom of the hill to catch her breath.

While Anniranni sat at the bottom of the hill, Mollymishi rattled along at top speed behind Dillip. The small Persian cat fled around the corner of the house. Dillip raced around the corner of the house and down the driveway after that small Persian cat. Mollymishi and the wee red wagon followed right behind. Mollymishi's hand held tight in Dillip's leash.

Mollymishi, and the wee red wagon headed like a chariot down the steep-downhill. Mollymishi hurled down the hill in the wee red wagon. The sidewalk sped by. The down hill wind blew her hair all around in the air. Mollymishi was the wildest-haired doll that ever rode that hill.

At the bottom of the steep-downhill, Anniranni sat wondering where Mollymishi, her wild-haired doll and her wee red wagon had gone. Then she heard a bright sound. It was the sound of the shiny silver wee red wagon wheels on the crumply sidewalk. Anniranni looked up.

There, galloping straight towards her was one small wide-eyed Persian cat, the Vevverly's dog Dillip, her wee red chariot wagon, and her beloved wild-haired doll Mollymishi.

Anniranni ran and ran away from her wild-haired doll and her wee red wagon.

She ran and ran past Sally Watermelon's, past Beefie Wellington's and down to her very own house.

Before Anniranni could run up her own front steps, that small Persian cat, Dillip, the wee red wagon, and Molly-mishi tumbled to a scalloping stop in the middle of her driveway. Mollymishi landed on her wild wild hair. She looked at Anniranni upsidedown.

"Well," said Annirani.

And she picked up Mollymishi and shook her until all her hair stood up wild again around her wide eyes.

Anniranni and Mollymishi left the wee red wagon tipped on its side in the middle of the driveway with its shiny silver wheels spinning in the wind.

They left Dillip, the brown-eyed dog, panting and sprawled at the top of the driveway on his stomach.

They left that wide-eyed small Persian cat beside the driveway clinging to a small bush.

And Anniranni and Mollymishi went inside to have two helpings of peas and quiet.